To Ginger,
Oti and Diggy

ISBN 0-439-05946-1

Copyright © 1997 by Charlotte Voake.
All rights reserved.
Published by Scholastic Inc., 555 Broadway, New York, NY 10012,
by arrangement with Candlewick Press.
SCHOLASTIC and associated logos are trademarks and/or registered
trademarks of Scholastic Inc.

12 11 10 9 8 7 6 5 4 3 2 1   9/9 0 1 2 3 4/0

Printed in the U.S.A.   08

First Scholastic printing, January 1999

This book was typeset in Calligraphic.
The pictures were done in watercolor and ink.

GINGER

Charlotte Voake

SCHOLASTIC INC.
New York Toronto London Auckland Sydney
Mexico City New Delhi Hong Kong

Ginger was a lucky cat.

He lived with
a little girl
who made him
delicious
meals

and gave him
a beautiful basket,

where he would curl up . . .

and close
his eyes.

Here he is,
fast asleep.

But here he is again,
WIDE AWAKE.

What's this?

A kitten!

"He'll be a nice new friend for you, Ginger," said the little girl.

But Ginger
didn't want a new friend,
especially one like this.
Ginger hoped the
kitten would
go away,

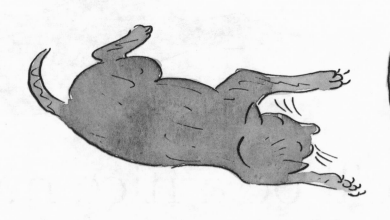

but he didn't.

Everywhere
Ginger went,
the kitten followed,
springing out
from behind
doors,

leaping onto Ginger's back,

even eating
Ginger's food!

What a naughty
kitten!

But what upset Ginger
more than anything
was that whenever
he got into his
beautiful basket,
the kitten always
climbed in too,

and
the little
girl didn't
do anything
about it.

So Ginger decided to leave home.

He went out
through the cat flap
and he didn't come back.

The kitten waited for a while,
then he got into
Ginger's basket.

It wasn't the same without Ginger.

The kitten
played
with some
flowers,

then he found
somewhere
to sharpen
his claws.

The little girl
found him on the table
drinking some milk.

"You naughty kitten!" she said.

"I thought you were with Ginger. Where is he anyway?"

She looked in Ginger's basket,

but of course he wasn't there.

"Perhaps he's eating his food," she said.

But Ginger wasn't there either.

"I hope he's not upset," she said.

"I hope he hasn't run away."

She put on her galoshes and went out into the garden, and that is where she found him;

a very wet,
sad, cold Ginger,
hiding under
a bush.

The little girl carried Ginger and the kitten inside. "It's a pity you can't be friends," she said.

She gave Ginger a special meal.

She gave the kitten
a little plate
of his own.

Then she tucked Ginger
into his own
warm basket.

All she could find for the kitten
to sleep in was a little tiny
cardboard box.

But the kitten
didn't mind, because
cats love cardboard boxes
(however small they are).

So when the little girl
went in to see
the two cats
again,

THIS is how she found them.

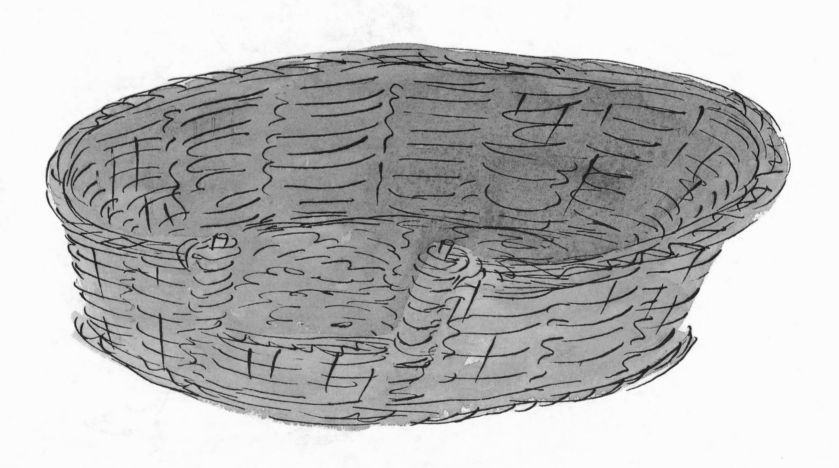

And now Ginger
and the naughty kitten
get along very well . . .

most of the time!